Disney

RAYA
AND
THE LAST DRAGON

THE GUARDIAN OF THE DRAGON GEM

Adapted by Suzanne Francis

Illustrated by Denise Shimabukuro and the Disney Storybook Art Team

A Random House PICTUREBACK® Book

Random House 🏠 New York

Published in the United States by Random House Children's Books, a division of Penguin Random House LLC, 1745 Broadway, New York, NY 10019,
and in Canada by Penguin Random House Canada Limited, Toronto, in conjunction with Disney Enterprises, Inc. Pictureback, Random House, and
the Random House colophon are registered trademarks of Penguin Random House LLC.

rhcbooks.com

ISBN 978-0-7364-4110-0
Printed in the United States of America
10 9 8 7 6 5 4 3 2 1

The moon glowed over the Land of Heart. While most people were drifting off to sleep, one young warrior was preparing for an important mission.

She was **determined** and strong. Her name was **Raya**.

Under the cover of night, Raya swiftly
darted across the palace grounds.
She made her way into the ancient

Dragon Temple.

Raya crept through the temple's winding tunnels. And then . . .
she paused. Her fingers ran across a strange groove in the wall.

"Looks like someone's trying to be clever," she whispered.

She reached into her bag and pulled out a small creature.

"All right, Tuk Tuk," said Raya, giving the creature a pat.
"Let's show 'em what clever *really* looks like."

Tuk Tuk curled into a ball and rolled down the hallway. His motion set off hidden traps! Nets sprang out everywhere, but Tuk Tuk stayed safely beneath each one. Raya smiled as she crawled behind him.

When they reached a circular door, she removed her shoes and stepped through.

Tuk Tuk stayed behind and watched as Raya continued.

As Raya entered a hidden chamber, she could feel the tingling buzz of magic in the air. She gasped as her eyes fell upon her target: the Dragon Gem. It floated above a pool of water.

Raya looked around suspiciously. "This feels too easy. . . ."

Suddenly, a warrior stepped out of the shadows. He stood between Raya and the Gem.

"I know it's your job to try and stop me, but . . . you won't," Raya said.

"Don't mistake spirit for skill, young one," he replied. "I promise you will not set foot on the Dragon Gem's inner circle. Not even a toe."

Raya sprang into action!
She leapt forward and attacked
the masked warrior.

Raya put up an excellent fight, but the masked warrior disarmed her. She froze as he held her at the point of his sheathed sword . . . and used it to tap her nose!

"BOOP," he said in a playful voice.

The warrior removed his mask.
"Like I said, not one foot on the inner
circle. You lost, Raya."
"Did I?" she said with her
eyebrows raised.
The two looked down to see . . .
Raya's toe on the inner circle!

"Hey. Don't beat yourself up too much, Chief Benja," Raya said with a smirk. "You gave it your best."

"I won't," Benja replied. "And it's either Father or *Ba* to you." He smiled with pride as he helped Raya to her feet. "You did good, dewdrop. You passed the test."

Raya took a deep breath and joined her father on the circle.
The Dragon Gem was even more dazzling than she had imagined.
"Wow," she said, awestruck.

"The spirit of Sisu."

Benja knelt before the Gem, and Raya followed suit.

"For generations, our family has sworn to protect the Gem, just as the Gem protects all of us," said Benja. **"Today, you will join in that legacy."**

He cupped his hands and dipped them into the glittering pool. Then he gently poured water onto Raya.

The drops of water glowed and began to float around her.

"Raya, Princess of Heart, my daughter," said Benja. "You are now a Guardian of the Dragon Gem."

Raya and her father looked proudly into each other's eyes.

As they turned to admire **the beauty of the Gem,** Raya planted the moment firmly in her mind, **determined to hold it forever.** She leaned against her father, and he wrapped his arm around her. The two felt happy, knowing that together they would do whatever it took to protect the **Dragon Gem.**

RAYA

TUK TUK

CHIEF BENJA

SISU (DRAGON FORM)

SISU (HUMAN FORM)

BOUN

UKA (ONGI)

PAN (ONGI)

DYAN (ONGI)

NOI

TONG

NAMAARI